JACK RUSSELL: Dog Detective

The Lying Postman

DARREL & SALLY ODGERS

SCHOLASTIC CANADA LTD.

New York   Toronto   London   Auckland   Sydney
Mexico City   New Delhi   Hong Kong   Buenos Aires

Scholastic Canada Ltd.
604 King Street West, Toronto, Ontario M5V 1E1, Canada

Scholastic Inc.
557 Broadway, New York, NY 10012, USA

Scholastic Australia Pty Limited
PO Box 579, Gosford, NSW 2250, Australia

Scholastic New Zealand Limited
Private Bag 94407, Greenmount, Auckland, New Zealand

Scholastic Children's Books
Euston House, 24 Eversholt Street, London NW1 1DB, UK

Library and Archives Canada Cataloguing in Publication
Odgers, Darrel
The lying postman / Darrel & Sally Odgers ; Janine Dawson, illustrator.

(Jack Russell, dog detective ; 4)
ISBN-13: 978-0-439-93799-3
ISBN-10: 0-439-93799-X

1. Dogs--Juvenile fiction. I. Odgers, Sally, 1957- II. Dawson, Janine
III. Title. IV. Series: Odgers, Darrel. Jack Russell, dog detective ; 4.
PZ7.O2374Ly 2007   j823'.92   C2006-905223-9

First published by Scholastic Press in 2005
Text copyright © Sally and Darrel Odgers, 2005
Cover design copyright © Lake Shore Graphics, 2005
Dog, Frisbee, courtesy of the Cansick family
Interior illustrations by Janine Dawson
Interior illustrations copyright © Scholastic Australia, 2005
All rights reserved.

6 5 4 3 2 1   Printed in Canada   06 07 08 09 10

Dear Readers,

The story you're about to
read is about me and my
friends and how we solved
the case of the Lying Postman. To save
time, I'll introduce us all to you now.
Of course, if you know us already, you
can trot off to Chapter One.

    I am Jack Russell, Dog Detective.
I live with my landlord, Sarge, in
Doggeroo. Sarge detects human-type
crimes. I detect the crimes that deal
with dogs. I'm a Jack Russell terrier, so
I am dogged and intelligent.

    Next door to Sarge and me live
Auntie Tidge and Foxy. Auntie Tidge is
lovely. She has dog biscuits. Foxy is not
lovely. He's a fox terrier (more or less).

He used to be a street dog and a thief, but he's reformed now. Auntie Tidge has even gotten rid of his fleas. Foxy sometimes helps me with my cases.

Uptown Lord Setter (Lord Red for short) lives in Uptown House with Caterina Smith. Lord Red means well, but he isn't very bright.

We have other friends and acquaintances in Doggeroo. These include Polly the dachshund, Jill Russell, the squekes, and Shuffle the pug. Then there's Fat Molly Cat from the Library.

That's all you need to know, so let's start Chapter One.

Yours doggedly,

Jack Russell—the detective with a nose for crime

The Yowling Basket

Foxy and I were digging a hole in Foxy's yard. Kitty Booker, the Doggeroo librarian, came through the gate, carrying a big basket.

"I smell food," said Foxy, and started to drool. Foxy will eat anything he can get.

I made a quick **nose map**.

<u>Jack's Map</u>

1. The beef bone Foxy had hidden under a bush.

2. The **special biscuits** Auntie Tidge makes.

3. Foxy's old boot.

4. Cat food.

5. Cat.

"It's Cat Crunchies," I said. "It's also Fat Molly."

Foxy bristled. "Where? Where?"

I *sniff-sniffed* the air. "She's in that basket with the Cat Crunchies," I said.

As Kitty Booker walked past us, Foxy growled at the basket.

The basket yowled back.

Jack's Facts

Baskets don't yowl.
Cats yowl.
So, baskets that yowl must have a cat inside.
This is a fact.

Foxy growled at the basket again. No terrier can see a basketful of cat in his **terrier-tory** and not take action. Before he could do anything about it, Auntie Tidge opened the door.

"Hello, Kitty!" said Auntie Tidge. "It *will* be nice to have Molly stay with me!"

Kitty Booker held out the yowling basket. "Thanks, **Miss Russell**. It's really kind of you to look after Molly while I go to the conference. I had asked Tina Boxer to take care of her, but now that she has her new dog, Ralf, she can't."

"It's no trouble at all," said Auntie Tidge.

Foxy growled, "It's going to be trouble for *me*." He glared at Kitty Booker and Auntie Tidge as she carried the basket into the house.

"Cheer up, Foxy," I said. "You can play **Cat-ch Cat**."

"**Dogwash!**" snapped Foxy. "Auntie Tidge won't let me!"

Jack's Facts

Where there are cats, there is cat food.
Cat food is good—even for dogs.
Dogs eat faster than cats.
This is a fact.

I reminded Foxy of this fact, and that cheered him up.

"I'm going to hide my old boot," he said. "And I'll bury my beef bone. And she's not sitting on my blanket. And she can't have any special biscuits."

"Cats don't eat special biscuits," I said. "They have their own tasty cat treats. It'll be all right. You'll see."

Just then, Sarge came home, so I scooted back into my own terrier-tory to **greet** him. Sarge is my landlord, and I don't want him to feel neglected.

Jack's Glossary

Nose map. *A way of storing information with the nose.*

Special biscuits. *Dog biscuits Auntie Tidge makes. They don't harm terrier teeth.*

Terrier-tory. *A territory owned by a terrier.*

Miss Russell. *I am Jack Russell. Sarge is Sergeant Russell. Auntie Tidge is Miss Russell.*

Jack's Glossary

Cat-ch Cat. *A game dogs play with cats.*

Dogwash. *Nonsense.*

Greet. *Standing on the hind legs and clutching a person with the paws while slurping them on the face.*

The Postman Game

Next morning, I was giving my
breakfast bowl a good polish with my
tongue when Foxy dragged his old
boot into my yard.

"You haven't been eating cat food,
have you?" I asked. (My **super-sniffer**
told me that he hadn't.)

Foxy dropped the boot. "No, and I
haven't had breakfast, either."

"That's pawful!" I said. "You're not
sick, are you? You're not dying?"

"It's Fat Molly's fault," grumbled
Foxy. "Kitty Booker has her on a diet."

"What does that have to do with you?"

"Auntie Tidge has put *me* on a diet, too!" snapped Foxy. "She won't give me special biscuits until I lose weight!"

Fat Molly came **pussyfooting** into my yard, waving her crooked tail. She sat down to lick herself.

Of course, I **Jack-yapped** at her. "Scat, cat!" I yapped. "Scat, fat cat!"

Fat Molly glared at me with her green eyes and flicked a ragged ear. She said something **terrier-ably** rude, with spits in it. Then she rolled on Foxy's old boot.

Foxy snarled.

Fat Molly **cat-apulted** to her feet and jumped onto the gatepost.

Foxy jumped up and down, barking insults.

Jack's Facts

Cats insult dogs.
Dogs insult cats.
The cats always start it, therefore it's
their fault.
This is a fact.

"Foxy Woxy? What's going on?"
Auntie Tidge came bustling into my yard.

Jack's Facts

*Humans always arrive after a cat
has been insulting.
Humans always arrive when a dog is
reacting.
Therefore, dogs get the blame.
This is a fact.*

I **Jack-jumped** into Auntie Tidge's
arms. I gave her a good swipe on the
face with my tongue and knocked her
glasses sideways. She loves it when I do
that.

Foxy glared at his boot. "Mine, mine,
mine!" he growled. "Mine, mine, mine."

"Foxy Woxy, no one wants your
boot." Auntie Tidge put me down and
picked up the boot. Foxy snatched it and

dragged it under a bush. "Mine, mine, mine."

I stared. Foxy has always been **paw-ssessive** about that boot, but being on a diet was making him worse.

Auntie Tidge saw Fat Molly sitting on the gate. "Poor Molly Wolly. Has naughty Foxy been rude to you?"

Molly meowed sadly. Auntie Tidge dragged Foxy and the boot from under the bush. She dropped them both over the little hedge. Then she took Fat Molly and went home.

I chewed my **squeaker-bone** for a while. I could still hear Foxy on the other side of the hedge muttering, "mine, mine, mine."

"Let's play the Postman Game," I suggested.

The postman was coming up the
street. Any minute, he'd rattle the
mailbox.

<u>Jack's Facts</u>

Postmen always rattle mailboxes.
Dogs bark when postmen rattle.
Postmen yell when dogs bark.
That's how you play the Postman Game.
This is a fact.

We'd been playing the game with
our postman for ages but that day
something went wrong.

Foxy barked. The postman yelled.
Foxy barked some more.

The postman should then come to
my gate. I would bark, and the postman

would yell at me. But this postman didn't play. Instead, he opened Foxy's gate and kicked Foxy. The postman wasn't *our* postman. It was a new one.

Foxy yelped with shock and ran to hide under Auntie Tidge's bed.

I didn't know it yet, but that was the start of the Case of the Lying Postman.

Jack's Glossary

Super-sniffer. *Jack's nose in super-tracking mode.*

Pussyfooting. *The way cats walk. Also known as catfooting.*

Jack-yap. *A loud, piercing yap made by a Jack Russell terrier.*

Terrier-ably. *Very.*

Cat-apult. *A very fast movement made by a cat when a terrier is barking at it.*

Jack-jump. *A sudden spring made by a Jack Russell terrier.*

Paw-ssessive. *The way some dogs get when someone tries to take away their belongings.*

Squeaker-bone. *Something for exercising a terrier's jaws. Not to be confused with a toy.*

The Lying Postman

When Foxy raced inside, Auntie Tidge came out. "What's going on?"

"Your dog tried to bite me," the postman lied.

"That's a lie!" I Jack-yapped.

Foxy's manners are **terrier-able**, but biting isn't part of the Postman Game.

"Foxy can't get out if the gate's shut," Auntie Tidge said. "So he *could not* have bitten you."

Jack's Facts

Terriers jump over.
Terriers burrow under.
Terriers push through.
Auntie Tidge doesn't know everything.
This is a fact.

"Did you open the gate?" Auntie Tidge asked.

"No!" snapped the postman. "That dog jumped up and tried to bite me."

"That's a lie!" I Jack-yapped again. I Jack-jumped a few times.

"That mongrel is trying to bite me too," said the postman, pointing at me.

"Nonsense," said Auntie Tidge. "Jack's just curious."

The postman grumbled past my

gate. I didn't bark again. He didn't play fair, and he didn't even know what kind of dog I was. He thought I was a *mongrel*!

Auntie Tidge thought he was wrong, too. She shook her head and went off to do her shopping.

I put my chin on my paws. There was **skulldoggery** afoot. I could smell it in the air.

"Jack Russell's the name, detection's the game," I said aloud, but how could I investigate this crime? There was nothing to investigate. I sat down to look at the facts.

1. The Crimes: kicking Foxy; lying to Auntie Tidge.
2. The **Pupetrator**: the postman.
3. The Method: kicking and lying.
4. The Opportunity: the postman had been passing our gates.
5. Possible Motive: hatred of dogs.

It all seemed clear to me. There was nothing to investigate.

The Case of the Lying Postman seemed dead in the water.

When Auntie Tidge had gone, Foxy slunk out of the house. My super-sniffer detected him on the other side of the hedge. He was muttering, "It's not fair. It's not fair. It's not fair."

"**Ig-gnaw** that lying postman, Foxy."

"You're not the one that got kicked,"

said Foxy. "You're not the one forced to go on a diet." Foxy's belly rumbled.

Fat Molly hopped onto the end of the fence and called Foxy something terrier-able, but he ig-gnawed her.

"I'd offer you some of my breakfast if I hadn't already eaten it," I said. "At least you'll get a good supper."

Foxy did get supper, but he wasn't **pawfully** pleased with it.

"Auntie Tidge gave me *carrots*," he snarled. "What does she think I am—a rabbit?"

"Carrots?" I was shocked. The thought of a rabbit that looked like Foxy was truly **terrier-fying**.

"Carrots and Cat Crunchies," moaned Foxy. His belly rattled again. "Fat Molly got Cat Crunchies, too.

Auntie Tidge fed her on top of the fridge."

That was mean of Auntie Tidge. How is a terrier expected to get his teeth into a cat's food if the cat is fed on top of the fridge?

<u>*Jack's Facts*</u>

Good dogs don't steal from people.
Good dogs don't steal from dogs.
Taking food from cats isn't stealing.
This is a fact.

"I'd offer you some of my supper,
but I already ate it," I said.

Being on a diet and having Fat Molly
to stay had a terrier-able effect on Foxy's
temper. Then being kicked by the lying
postman was the **last paw**. Foxy said he
was going to get revenge.

"Revenge on whom?" I asked

"Revenge on *everybody*," Foxy
growled.

Jack's Glossary

Terrier-able. *Very bad.*

Skulldoggery. *Bad things concerning dogs.*

Pupetrator. *A criminal who does things to dogs.*

Ig-gnaw. *Ignore, but done by dogs.*

Pawfully. *Very; awfully.*

Terrier-fying. *Frightening.*

Last paw. *Like the last straw, but happening to dogs.*

Foxy's Revenge

When Foxy said everybody, he meant
everybody. He even snarled at Auntie
Tidge.

I was shocked. "Don't you snarl at
Auntie Tidge!" I said.

"All right," said Foxy. "I'll ig-gnaw
her instead."

That shocked me even more.

Foxy got his revenge on Fat Molly.
He **terrier-ized** her by walking slowly
up to her and muttering under his
breath. Foxy stalked her like this every
time Fat Molly appeared.

<u>Jack's Facts</u>

Cats are expert stalkers.
Dogs hate being stalked by cats.
Cats hate being stalked by dogs even
more.
This is a fact.

"Stop that, Foxy," I said. "Stalking will make you even hungrier."

Foxy ig-gnawed me. That was his revenge on me.

"*I* haven't done anything to you!" I said.

Foxy went and squatted over his old boot. In a few minutes I heard him muttering, "You'd think a greedy Jack would share his breakfast with a hungry pal."

I *would* have shared my breakfast with Foxy if I hadn't been hungry myself. When Auntie Tidge had stopped giving Foxy special biscuits, she stopped giving them to me, too!

Foxy got his revenge on the lying postman. He lurked behind the gate and yapped and snapped when the postman rattled the mailbox.

The postman threw Auntie Tidge's letters over the gate.

"That dog next door is savage," he said to Sarge, who was just on his way to work.

Sarge laughed. "Savage?" He raised his voice over Foxy's yapping. "Foxy isn't savage."

"It is savage," lied the lying postman. "It should be tied up."

"But he's in a fenced yard," said Sarge.

"It should be tied up. I've already been bitten by one dog in this town. That one next door tried it, too. If you don't do something about it, I'll call Ranger Jack."

While the lying postman was lying to Sarge, I made a quick nose map.

Jack's Map

1. Empty breakfast bowl.

2. Foxy's old boot.

3. Fat Molly.

4. The lying postman.

5. Sarge.

6. Lord Red.

Lord Red? Because Foxy was
ig-gnawing me, I needed company. Lord
Red might have more hair than brains,
but he's still a pal. I Jack-jumped to look
over the gate.

The lying postman sprang backward.
"That mongrel should be tied up, too!"
he said, pointing at me.

"Jack is only looking over the gate,"
explained Sarge. "Now, can you describe
the dog that you claim *did* bite you? If
it's running loose, Ranger Jack will take
it to the pound."

"How should I know what sort of
dog it was? I tell you, it bit me! Look!"

The lying postman showed a rip in his uniform jacket. "You can see the marks."

"Nasty rip you have there," agreed Sarge. "I need details about the dog. Drop in at the station later and give me the facts."

The lying postman gave me a nasty look. He called me a terrier-able name and pedaled away.

Jack's Glossary

Terrier-ize. _To frighten, done by a terrier._

Red Is Upsettered

I Jack-jumped again to make sure the
lying postman had gone. Lord Red
was prancing up the street toward
him like a hairy shampoo model.

As Red passed the lying postman,
the postman's bike swerved. Red
yelped, spun around, and tore off the
way he'd come.

"Red!" I called. "Halt in the name
of the paw!"

Red kept on running, so I left the
yard (never mind how) and ran after
him.

I needed to find out what had **upsettered** him.

We ran past Dora Barkins's house. The three squekes were yipping in their yard. We ran past the library and up to the flea market. I caught Red on the hill. He didn't stop when I Jack-yapped, so I Jack-jumped and grabbed his tail in my teeth.

"Ow-wow-wowwwww!" howled Red. He spun around three times, so fast my **Jack-jaws** lost their grip. He sat down and put his paw on his tail.

After *that*, he spotted me. "Jack? Where did you come from, Jack? Jack, I just had a horrible thing happen. Some thing grabbed my tail! I think it was a **dognapper**. Will you take the case, Jack? Will you?"

My ears had turned inside out when I lost my grip, so I shook them the right way out.

"Calm down, Red," I ordered.

"A dognapper grabbed my tail!" repeated Red.

"That was me," I said. "I had to stop you."

Red jumped up, but he had his paw on his own tail, so he fell down again. "Why are you trying to dognap me, Jack?"

I groaned.

"Nobody is trying to dognap you," I said.

"Are you sure?" said Red.

"Quite sure," I said. "Red, I need to ask you something."

"Are you going to **interrier-gate** me, Jack? Are you on a case?"

"Yes," I said. "The Case of the Lying Postman. Why were you running up our street?"

"I wanted to see you, Jack," said Red. "You're my best friend."

"Then why did you run back down our street instead of coming to my gate?"

"The dognapper on the bike was riding toward me," said Red. "It upsettered me, so I was running back to Caterina Smith. Caterina Smith says I can't let dognappers get me."

"For the last time, Red, no one is trying to dognap you!"

"Okay," said Red. "Why did the dognapper ride his bike toward me, then?"

"He's not a dognapper. He's a postman," I said.

Red looked confused. "Postmen don't chase dogs, Jack. Dogs chase postmen."

"This postman hates dogs," I said. "He's been telling lies about Foxy and me."

"But that's pawful!" said Red.

"Exactly," I said. "He's a lying postman. Telling lies is what liars do."

"Foxy lies," said Red. "He tells Auntie Tidge he hasn't been fed when he has."

Jack's Facts

Dogs are hunters.
Telling their people they haven't been fed is just another form of hunting.
Therefore lying about food isn't really lying.
This is a fact.

I explained this to Red.

"Oh," said Red. "I'm going hunting, then." He jumped up and started galloping up the hill.

"Red!" I Jack-yapped, but Red had gone.

Jack's Glossary

Upsettered. *Bothered and upset a setter.*

Jack-jaws. *The splendid set of jaws owned by a Jack Russell.*

Dognapper. *Someone who steals dogs.*

Interrier-gate. *Official questioning, done by a terrier.*

Paw-Leash Work

Since Red had **desettered** me, I had to
find someone else to interrier-gate.
This meant heavy **paw-leash work**.
But because Foxy was ig-gnawing me,
I had no one to help me.

I started by going down to the
reserve to interrier-gate Shuffle the
pug, who lives with Walter Barkly. I
trotted up to Shuffle's yard and asked
pawmission to enter his territory.

Jack's Facts

Polite dogs always ask pawmission before
entering someone else's territory.
It is especially polite if the dog is larger
than the polite dog.
This has nothing to do with being afraid
of larger dogs.
This is a fact.

Shuffle didn't know anything about
postmen. Walter Barkly always picks up
his letters at the post office.

"Do you know who might have
bitten the postman?" I asked.

"Foxy," said Shuffle. "He threatened
to bite me once. I was terrier-ized."

"That was because you sat on his old
boot," I said.

I left Shuffle and went across the river to visit Polly the dachshund, who lives with Gloria Smote. Polly was **daching** about with Jill Russell, who lives with Jack and Jill Johnson near the train station.

"What do you want, Jack?" Polly asked.

"I'm on a case," I explained. "There's a lying postman at large. He said Foxy bit him. Foxy didn't. He said I tried to bite him. I didn't. He rode his bike at Red and upsettered him. He said another dog bit him. It didn't. He—"

"How do you know it didn't?" demanded Jill Russell. She poked me with her nose. She always does that.

"Because he's a lying postman!" I said.

"Even lying postmen don't lie about everything," said Jill.

Time to get down to business, I
thought. "Answer in the name of the
paw," I said. "Did either of you bite the
lying postman?"

"Of paws not!" snapped Polly. "The
only thing I bite is the food Gloria
Smote gives me."

"What about you, Jill Russell?" I
continued doggedly.

Jill Russell told me to go and play with Ralf Boxer. "He's just your type," she said.

Boxer! That gave me paws for thought. Where had I heard that name before? I couldn't remember, so I headed off to interrier-gate the squekes.

I might as well have saved my time. The squekes were squeking around in Dora Barkins's yard as usual, yipping and nipping one another.

"Did one of you squekes bite the lying postman?" I demanded.

The squekes yipped at me. It couldn't have been one of them that had bitten the postman. He said that only one dog had bitten him. The squekes operate as a team. Either all three had bitten him or none of them had. Besides, I've never been absolutely sure that squekes are dogs. They smell like dogs, but maybe they're really **dogbots**.

I went doggedly on around Doggeroo. None of the dogs I interrier-gated had bitten the lying postman, although some of them said he had lied and said they'd tried. I didn't meet any boxers. Finally, I went home.

Nothing had changed. Foxy was still ig-gnawing me. Auntie Tidge still wasn't making special biscuits. Sarge was still away. Fat Molly was licking herself on the gatepost.

Then I remembered where I'd heard Ralf Boxer's name before. Kitty Booker had said that Fat Molly couldn't stay with Tina Boxer because of her new dog, Ralf.

So, what did I know about Ralf
Boxer?

1. He was a dog.
2. He was the reason Fat Molly
   couldn't stay with Tina Boxer.
3. He was probably a boxer.
4. Kitty Booker knew him.
5. Jill Russell said he was "just my
   type."

That wasn't enough for me to make
an arrest. If I interrier-gated Fat Molly,
she'd probably cat-apult onto the roof
and start **cat-erwauling**. Then Auntie
Tidge would blame me.

Instead, I went back toward Uptown
House to ask Red about Ralf Boxer. Red
is not the brightest biscuit in the box, but
he goes everywhere and knows everyone.

Jack's Glossary

Desettered. *Desertion, done by a setter.*

Paw-leash work. *Detection done by a dog detective.*

Pawmission. *Permission, given by a dog.*

Daching. *The way dachshunds get about.*

Dogbots. *Robotic dogs.*

Cat-erwauling. *A horrible noise made by a cat.*

Red ALert

I trotted back past my house and Foxy's place, turned right where the three squekes live, and crossed the overpass. Then I ran into trouble. Ranger Jack was on the prowl.

Don't ask me why Doggeroo Dog Control Officer Johnny Wolf calls himself Ranger Jack. Maybe he thinks it's a snappy name.

Ranger Jack was talking to someone, and I stopped to make a nose map.

Jack's Map

1. A hot dog wrapper someone had dropped.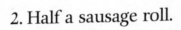

2. Half a sausage roll.

3. A dogbiscuit.

My belly rumbled. Detecting was
making me hungry. I needed a biscuit
break.

Sniff-sniff. Sniff-sniff. I started
sneaking toward the source of the
biscuit scent.

Sniff-sniff. Sniff- Oops! Now I
smelled something else, mixed with the
dog biscuits.

4. Ranger Jack.

5. The lying postman.

I Jack-yapped with surprise. Big
mistake.

"That's the mongrel that tried to bite
me!" yelled the lying postman. "Just after
the other mongrel tried to bite me and

before the big red dog attacked me!
Nearly knocked me off my bike."

"That's Sergeant Russell's Jack," said
Ranger Jack.

"He said it never left the yard!"
sneered the lying postman.

"That's a lie!" I Jack-yapped.

"The dogs of Doggeroo are out of
control," said the lying postman. "I
demand you *do* something."

Ranger Jack sighed. "I'll speak to
Caterina Smith. She has the only big red
dog I know, but Red wouldn't attack
anyone. You're right about something,
though. The dogs shouldn't be running
around loose." He pulled a dog biscuit
out of his pocket and held it out. "Hi,
Jack. Come on, boy."

I was glad Foxy wasn't with me. Foxy

is anyone's friend for a dog biscuit, but Jack Russells are made of sterner stuff.

I Jack-yapped again, dodged Ranger Jack, and ran to Uptown House.

I shot under Lord Red's hedge. "Red alert! Red alert! Hide!" I Jack-yapped.

Jack's Facts

Polite dogs always ask pawmission before entering someone else's territory.
It is especially polite if the dog is larger than the polite dog.
In an emergency, even a polite dog might ig-gnaw this rule.
This is a fact.

Lord Red had been racing about as usual. He skidded to a stop. His tail was whirling around like a propeller.

"Are we playing Hide-the-Jack, are we? Are weeeee?"

"Red alert!" I panted. "The lying postman is blackening your name. He told Ranger Jack you attacked him!"

"I didn't, Jack. I didn't! I wouldn't!" Red yelped. "Caterina Smith says dogs that attack get sent to the pouuunnnnd!"

"Be quiet!" I yapped. "They're coming."

Red and I burrowed under a bush, just before Ranger Jack and the lying postman knocked on the front door.

Caterina Smith opened the door. "Hello, Ranger Jack. Is there a problem?"

"Caterina, I'm sorry to tell you this, but the postman says a red setter and a Jack Russell attacked him. You have a

setter, and we saw Sarge's Jack heading
this way."

Caterina Smith laughed. "Lordie
doesn't attack people. He's here, but I
haven't seen Jack."

"Make sure your dog is here, please,"
said Ranger Jack.

"Of course." Caterina Smith called, "Lordie, *Lordie*! Lordieeeeee!"

Red quivered, but I had my Jack-jaws on his tail. "Red! We're hiding!"

"But Caterina Smith is calling!" whined Red.

I had to act fast. "Red, do you know a dog named Ralf Boxer?"

"Of paws!" said Red. "He lives in the empty-house-that-had-had-rats."

"Now we have a lead," I said. "If Ralf Boxer is the one that bit the lying postman, this is all his fault."

Red Herring

Red and I snuck out of Red's garden and ran to the old-house-that-had-had-rats. I made a quick nose map.

Jack's Map

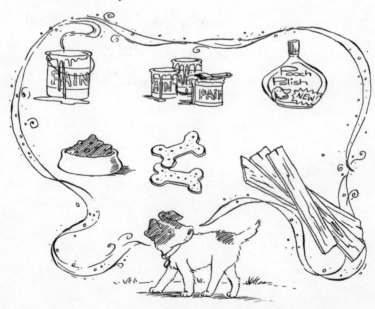

1. Paint.

2. More paint.

3. Pooch Polish.

4. Dog food.

5. Dog biscuits.

6. New timber.

It *did* smell different. I sneezed. The paint upset my super-sniffer, but there wasn't a hint of a rat. It looked different, too. There was a brand-new wooden fence. A person was painting the porch.

"That's Tina Boxer," said Red as the

person went into the house. He got up and rested his front paws on the top of the new fence. "I like Tina Boxer. She has dog biscuits." He began to sniff along toward the biscuit smell.

"Where—" I began, but before I got my question out, Red suddenly yelped and desettered me.

"My paw! My paw! My poor gnawed paw!" I heard him howling as he limped away on three paws.

"Red!" I Jack-yapped, but he was out of sight. I had a suspect to interrier-gate. And now it looked as if the suspect had bitten Red's paw.

I *sniff-sniffed*. The lying postman had been here, but not today. That made sense if Ralf Boxer had really bitten him. I hoped Ralf Boxer wasn't too big. Jack

Russells are scared of nothing, but it's pawfully stupid to look for trouble.

<u>*Jack's Facts*</u>

Jack Russells are not big dogs.
They are exactly the right size.
Therefore, any dog bigger than a Jack
Russell is too big.
This is a fact.

I knew my way around the empty-house-that-had-had-rats, from when I solved the Dog Den Mystery. I could order Ralf Boxer to report for interrier-gation, but what if he ig-gnawed me? What if he gnawed *my* paw? Or even gnawed *me*?

I *sniff-sniffed,* to see if I could detect

Ralf Boxer. He couldn't be far away, since he'd just bitten Red.

"Ralf Boxer?" I called politely. I put my nose under the fence. There was only a small gap, just enough for my Jack-jaws and super-sniffer to fit through. "Ralf Boxer?" I repeated. "Are you there?"

I *sniff-sniffed* right along the fence, but I couldn't smell a big dog.

And that wasn't all. Why didn't Ralf Boxer challenge me? Why didn't he threaten to rip my legs off and use them as toothpicks? Could Ralf Boxer be a terrier-able *coward*?

But wait. He *had* bitten Red, just for putting his paws on the fence.

I *sniff-sniffed* all along the fence. I decided to try a few Jack-jumps.

I bounced up like a **Jack-in-the-box**.

I was at the top of my jump when the smallest dog I've ever seen came out through the **dog door**. It was smaller than the rats that used to live in there. It would have fit into Sarge's coffee mug.

It spotted me at the top of my Jack-jump and came skittering over to the fence, yapping loudly.

"Go away, big dog! Go away! This is *my* **Chihuahua-tory**!"

I tried not to laugh. Small dogs don't like to be laughed at by big dogs, and

this was a very small dog. To this small dog, I was a big dog!

"Hi, pup. Does Ralf Boxer live here?" I asked.

"I am Ralf Boxer," said the small dog. "And *don't* call me 'pup'!"

"You can't be Ralf Boxer!"

"Why can't I?" A pointy little nose the size of a cherry pit jammed itself against mine and *sniff-sniffed*.

"Because you're not a boxer."

"Why would I be a boxer?"

"Then why are you called Ralf Boxer?"

"That's my name, not what I am. You're not called Jack Russell, are you?"

"Jack Russell's the name, detection's the game," I said.

"Oh." Ralf Boxer stared at me. "I'm coming out. Wait there."

Jack's Glossary

Jack-in-the-box. *A Jack in jumping-jack mode.*

Dog door. *A door especially for dogs.*

Chihuahua-tory. *A territory owned by a Chihuahua.*

interrier-gation

Ralf Boxer crawled under the gate. He looked like a half-grown rat. His hair was so fine I could see the skin underneath. He was trying to raise his hackles.

Jack's Facts

Most dogs have hackles.
Some dogs have hackles that make other dogs laugh.
Dogs like that should not raise their hackles.
This is a fact.

"What do you want, Jack?" he yipped.

"Do you know Lord Red?" I asked.

"Of paws. He came with Caterina
Smith to have coffee with Tina Boxer.
He's silly. He thought I was a mouse."

"Is that why you bit him?"

Ralf stared at me. "I didn't. Why

would I want to bite Lord Red? He's covered with hair!"

"Didn't you bite his paw just now when he put it over the fence?"

Ralf gave me a sarcastic look. "How would I do that, Jack?"

I looked at the fence. "Maybe you jumped up?"

Ralf Boxer sniffed. "Look, Jack. You are four times as tall as me. Even you can't jump as high as my fence."

"So you didn't bite Lord Red just now," I **pawsisted**.

"I didn't know Lord Red was here."

"He isn't," I said.

Ralf gave me a funny look. "Have you been eating bad biscuits, Jack? You don't seem quite right in the head. First you say—"

"Stop!" I ordered. "Lord Red *was* here. Something bit his paw and he ran home. I thought it was you. Because I thought you were the dog that bit the lying postman. Since you can't be that dog, I'll be leaving. Thank you for helping with my inquiries."

"I *am* the dog that bit the postman," said Ralf.

"I don't understand. You—you *what*?"

"I did bite the postman," said Ralf. "He called me a nasty little brat and tried to kick me, so I bit him."

I was terrier-ably impressed. Ralf Boxer was the smallest dog I'd ever seen, and he'd started all this fuss!

"You do realize the lying postman is telling lies about the dogs in Doggeroo because of you?" I said. "He thinks we're all out to get him. That means he's out to get us."

Ralf giggled.

"It's not funny!" I snapped. "Ranger Jack is after us." Then I remembered something. "How did you reach to bite the postman's jacket?"

"I didn't," said Ralf. "I bit his boot."

"You bit his boot?"

Ralf Boxer bristled. "What do you expect, Jack? I'm a Chihuahua."

My head was spinning. "Jill Russell said you were my kind of dog, and you're not," I said.

"Are you intelligent, loyal, lively, and brilliant in every way?" demanded Ralf Boxer.

"Yes," I said.

"Then I'm your kind of dog."

"But Kitty Booker said Tina Boxer couldn't look after Fat Molly because of you!"

Ralf Boxer had been looking pleased with himself, but now his eyes bugged out with terror. "Did you say *Fat Molly*? I *hate* Fat Molly! Fat Molly wants to eat me!" He was quivering like a cupful of jelly.

"Fat Molly couldn't stay here because *she* would attack *you*?" I said. "I thought it was the other way around. Maybe some other things are the other way around, too. You say you bit the lying postman on the boot. He says he was bitten in the jacket. You say you didn't bite Red at all. Red said his paw was bitten . . . and that means—"

"It means someone else must have bitten Lord Red *and* the lying postman's jacket," said Ralf Boxer.

"Or something else," I said.

I was about to continue the interrier-gation when Ralf Boxer looked past me and yelped. He dived back under the gate and vanished.

Ranger Jack and Sarge were coming around the corner with the lying postman.

"Jack? What are *you* doing here?" demanded Sarge.

"I told you so! This dog is *not* in its yard," said the lying postman, and he pounced on me.

Jack's Glossary

Pawsisted. *Kept doggedly on.*

The End of
the Case

There's only one thing to do when you're caught red-pawed out of your yard, and that's to practice **Jack-straction**.

I Jack-yapped and Jack-jumped as hard as I could.

The lying postman had to let me go. I sailed over the fence and landed inside the yard.

"Get out of my Chihuahua-tory, Jack!" yapped Ralf Boxer, and bit me on the toe.

I hardly noticed. In that few seconds, while I was sailing through the air, I'd spotted a long splinter of wood sticking out of the top of the new fence. Stuck to it was a scrap of the lying postman's uniform and a tuft of Red's hair.

The last piece of the puzzle had fallen into place, and I'd solved the Case of the Lying Postman.

Now all I had to do was to get Sarge to see the evidence.

In a **pawfect** world, I could have pointed my super-sniffer at the evidence. But, what really happened was this.

1. Sarge ordered me to come out of Ralf Boxer's yard.
2. I Jack-yapped and Jack-jumped as close to the evidence as I could.
3. Every time Sarge tried to grab me, I Jack-jumped back.

4. Finally, Sarge had to lean right
   over the fence.

You can guess what happened next.

"Ouch!" yelled Sarge. He shot back
from the fence, leaving a piece of his
jacket on the splinter.

That's when Sarge noticed the piece
of the lying postman's uniform already
there. He picked it off and held it up to
Ranger Jack and the lying postman.

"Could *that* be what bit you, do you
think?" he asked, pointing at the splinter.

Of paws, the lying postman tried to
lie, but the evidence was there.

"I'm *sure* there was a dog," he said.

Sarge bent over the fence again and
picked up Ralf Boxer. "This one,
maybe?" he asked.

Ralf Boxer growled and snapped at the lying postman's nose.

Ranger Jack laughed.

The lying postman called Ralf Boxer something terrier-able and marched away. We never saw him again.

Ralf Boxer believes he scared the lying postman away from Doggeroo. I know it was my brilliant detective work that really made him leave.

That was the end of the Case of the Lying Postman. Sarge took me home, and on the way we met Kitty Booker, with a yowling basket under her arm.

Fat Molly was going home.

"Scat, fat cat!" I yapped, and Fat Molly said something really rude in Cat.

"Well, Foxy," I said when we got together later in the afternoon. "Are you

still ig-gnawing me?"

Foxy ig-gnawed me.

Just then, Lord Red came tearing up
the street. "Jack, Jack, my poor gnawed
paw is well again! Caterina Smith made it
better and gave me a whole pile of beef

bones! Are you coming to Uptown House to help me hide them, Jack? Are you?"

"Why not?" I said.

I left the yard (never mind how) and trotted off with Red.

As we were turning the corner, Foxy tore past us and vanished in a cloud of dust.

After that, I had a new challenge. How could Red and I hide the bones before Foxy stole them all?

Jack's Glossary

Jack-straction. *Distraction, done by a Jack.*

Pawfect. *Perfect, but about dogs. If it was cats, it would be "purrfect."*
